Salt Boy

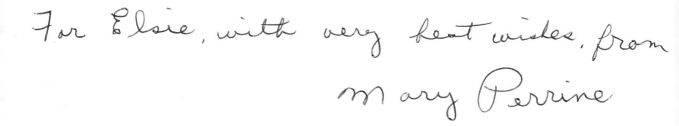

Salt Boy

MARY PERRINE

Illustrated by Leonard Weisgard

1968

HOUGHTON MIFFLIN COMPANY BOSTON

For the children
who have taught me how much courage
people can have

Salt Boy

Salt Boy

The thing Salt Boy wanted only his father could give him. But asking for it, Salt Boy thought, might make his father be against it. Then, one morning, he asked for it.

He was in the trees getting wood for his mother's fire, when he saw his father coming with a rope to begin the training of the black horse.

His heart began to jump in a funny way, like a grasshopper, and he went to the bent tree, where he could stand not far from the black horse, and watch his father when he threw the rope.

The black horse was eating grass. Salt Boy's father walked quietly, and the black horse didn't hear him until he was near. Then, suddenly, its ears went up, and its head, and it began to dance away backwards.

Still walking quietly, Salt Boy's father threw the rope. With no sound, it went high over the black horse's ears, and slid down easily around its neck.

The black horse stood there, surprised, and shook its head as if a fly had bothered it. Keeping the rope tight, Salt Boy's father went close to the black horse, and talked to it, and stroked it with kindness. Then he untied the rope, and let the black horse go.

It was then Salt Boy went to his father and, hiding his face, almost, with the wood in his arms, said it. "My father, will you teach me sometime to rope the black horse?"

Without answering, his father started to their hogan, and Salt Boy went behind him. Without words, they crossed the red sand of the mesa top, and went down the black rocks below.

When they came to the pen for Salt Boy's mother's sheep, his father stopped and waited until Salt Boy was beside him. Then he spoke. "I have said it before, my son, that you must never rope the sheep of your mother."

Salt Boy wanted to hide from his father the shame on his face, and he looked at the ground, and turned a rock over with his toe.

He was thinking that his father must know, then, what he had done in the canyon when he took his mother's sheep for grass.

Then his father spoke again. "Maybe, my son," he said, "when your years are more I will teach you to rope the black horse."

Salt Boy and his father looked at each other in a way that was strong, and Salt Boy knew his father had asked without words for a promise, and without words Salt Boy had given it to him. That promise he thought he would keep.

In the morning, Salt Boy took his mother's sheep to the canyon for grass.

Near the wash at the bottom of the canyon the grass was green and deep, and the sheep ran to it, pushing against each other. When the sheep ran, the lamb that was littlest lost its mother and cried, "M-a-a." Salt Boy lifted it, and carried it with gentleness to its mother.

There was a tall flat rock by the grass where the sheep were, and Salt Boy climbed up on it. From there he could watch the sheep, and if he turned around and leaned over, he could see the cave that held that thing he had found.

He remembered the morning he had found it there. At first, when he saw it in the cave, he had thought it was a snake, and he had felt it with a long stick, and moved it, and turned it over. When the stick told him it was a thing without life, he had gone close to it, and put his hand on it. It wasn't until then he had known it was a rope.

He had pulled it carefully and slowly out of the darkness in the cave. Then he had sat on the ground and looked at it, and felt it, and held it. He had done that with it all day, until it was time to take his mother's sheep back up the canyon path. Then he had coiled it very slowly, and put it back in the cave's darkness.

After that morning he had taken the rope out of the cave many times. He had learned to tie it well, and he had learned to throw it without missing over the round gray rocks that were in the canyon.

Then, one time when the rope was in his hands, and he was getting ready to throw it over a round gray rock, a sheep had come near, and suddenly he had thrown it over the sheep's head.

Now Salt Boy sat on the rock that was tall and flat. He was thinking about that first time, and he was thinking about how many times after that he had thrown the rope over the heads of other sheep of his mother. And he was thinking about yesterday, and the promise he had given his father.

He might have stayed there longer, but his legs hurt from the rock that was tall and flat, and after a while he jumped to the ground. Then, without planning it, he went to the cave where the rope was hidden.

He could see it in the cave's darkness, and he leaned down to take it out. Just then a noise began coming from the sky. Black clouds were in it, and wind was coming from it. Then gray rain began to come, and soon gray rain was everywhere.

Salt Boy started to the sheep. Heavy wind stood against him, and to walk he had to hold big rocks and pull himself.

At last, that way, he came to the grass by the wash. The sheep were afraid, and were standing close to one another. They were stiff, like things made from wood. Quickly Salt Boy counted — first the sheep, and then the lambs. One lamb was missing! The littlest lamb was gone!

Salt Boy looked at the wash, which was near. It was full of water that was moving fast, like a strong horse running.

Something was in the water by the flat rock, and Salt Boy leaned over to see it better. It was the littlest lamb, and it was kicking and trying to stand. But it kept slipping and falling, and then the water carried it.

Salt Boy tried to go in the water to help the littlest lamb, but the wind pushed him, and he fell. To get out, he crawled on his knees.

The rope that was in the cave, he knew then, was the only way he could save the littlest lamb.

Gray rain was still coming, and wind, and he held big rocks and pulled himself, until he was near the cave. He crawled to it and got the rope, and then he held big rocks and pulled himself again, until he was back by the wash.

He tied the rope as fast as he could, and threw it. He missed, and threw again. This time it went over the head of the littlest lamb.

Salt Boy pulled the rope slowly, and carefully, until the littlest lamb was out of the water.

He lifted it, and held it in his arms. It was lying very still, but when Salt Boy put his face close to it, he could feel the beating of its heart.

Something — maybe a sound — made him look around. His father was standing behind him. His father stayed there for a while, and then he said with quietness, "I watched, my son, while you saved the littlest lamb of your mother."

He still didn't go.

Salt Boy held the littlest lamb and waited. Then his father said, "Tomorrow, my son, I will teach you to rope the black horse."

31